GRUMBLY BUNNIES

GRUMBLY BUNNIES

Willy Welch
illustrated by Tammie Lyon

▚▚ Charlesbridge

2009 First paperback edition
Text copyright © 2003 by Willy Welch
Illustrations copyright © 2000 by Tammie Lyon

Published by Charlesbridge
85 Main Street
Watertown, MA 02472
(617) 926-0329
www.charlesbridge.com

Library of Congress Cataloging-in-Publication Data
Welch, Willy.
[Grumpy bunnies]
Grumbly bunnies / Willy Welch ; illustrated by Tammie Lyon.
p. cm.
Previous ed. pub. under title: Grumpy bunnies.
Summary: Three little bunnies have a busy day, from breakfast to school to
time to sleep and dream.
ISBN 978-1-58089-087-8 (softcover)
[1. Stories in rhyme. 2. Rabbits—Fiction. 3. Day—Fiction.
4. Schools—Fiction.] I. Lyon, Tammie, ill. II. Title.
PZ8.3.W44   Gp 2009
[E]—dc22   2008031685

Printed in China
(sc) 10 9 8 7 6 5 4 3 2 1

Illustrations done in watercolors
Display type and text type set in Ad Lib
Color separated, printed, and bound by Toppan Printing Company
Production and design by *The Kids at Our House*

Grumbly Bunnies
in the morning,

crusty eyes and groggy yawns,

stumble bumbling in the closet,
struggle putting school clothes on.

Moody Bunnies
chomping breakfast,
lumpy oatmeal,
soggy bread,
slumping in their table places,
frumpy faces,
sulky heads.

Grouchy Bunnies
riding buses,
knobby seats on bumpy streets,

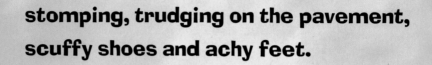

stomping, trudging on the pavement,
scuffy shoes and achy feet.

**Spunky Bunnies
on the playground,
jungle gymming,**

tossing balls,
muddy running,
grungy sneakers,
coming when the teacher calls.

Sunny Bunnies
munching lunches,
yummy crumbs of sandwich things,

in their classes,
learning lessons,
numbers,
dancing,
songs and sings.

Snuggly Bunnies after school,
huggy mommy,
holding hands,
tummies hungry, cracker snacking,
laps and stories,
fairylands.

Sudsy Bunnies bubble bathing,

comfy jammies,
silky sheets,
tucking blankets, snuggly kisses,
Drowsy Bunnies go to sleep.

Snoozy Bunnies
snuffle snoring,
flopping in their featherbeds.

**Happy Bunnies
slumber dreaming—**

there's another day ahead.